Vampire School
Show
and Yell

First published in Great Britain in 2011
by Boxer Books Limited.

www.boxerbooks.com

Based on an original idea by Chris Harrison
Text copyright © 2011 Peter Bently
Illustrations copyright © 2011 Chris Harrison

The illustrations were prepared using biro and watercolour paints.
The text is set in Blackmoor Plain and Adobe Caslon.

ISBN 978-1-907967-12-2

3 5 7 9 10 8 6 4 2

Printed in Great Britain

All of our papers are sourced from managed forests and renewable resources.

MORE FANGTASTIC Vampire School titles to enjoy!

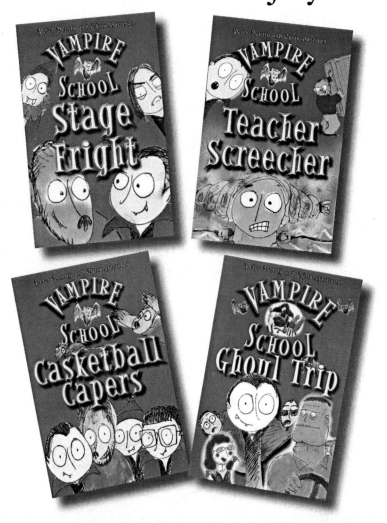

Coming soon to Vampire School

Monster Chef

Vampire School
Show and Yell

Written by Peter Bently

Illustrated by Chris Harrison

Boxer Books

Contents

Chapter 1
The Battlesnake

'Evening, Lee,' said Mum.
'Come on, time to get up!
It's twenty to eight.'

''S too early,' grumbled Lee
Price sleepily. 'S not eight
o'clock yet!'

He turned over in his coffin
and yanked the duvet over
his head.

'But you need to get Britney ready,' said Mum, peeling the duvet off him again. 'You're taking her to school, tonight, remember?'

Lee's eyes opened wide.

'Oh yeah,' he yawned.
'I forgot.'

Lee leapt out of bed. Miss Gargoyle, his teacher at St

Orlok's Primary School for young vampires, had asked everyone to bring in their pets tonight for a special show-and-yell lesson. She was going to give a prize for the creepiest creature and Lee was sure that his new pet Britney was going to win it. He wanted to make sure her cage was spotless.

Lee quickly got dressed and hurried down to breakfast.

'Now don't forget to keep Britney's cage locked,' said Mum, as Lee chomped his Mournflakes.

'And if you do take her out, make sure she's always on her lead,' chipped in Dad. 'We don't want any complaints about missing pets!'

'Or terrified Fangless people,' said Mum. 'Otherwise Britney will have to go back to the Monster Rescue Centre.'

'Don't worry, Mum,' said Lee.
'I'll keep a close eye on her.'

Dad slurped down his coffee.

'Ugh!' he winced. 'I hate
decoffinated. Right, Lee, time
to go. You get Britney, I'll get
the Vamp-Wagon.'

Normally Lee just turned into a bat and flew to St Orlok's. But tonight he had to take Britney's cage so Dad was driving him in their old Vamp-Wagon camper van.

'Bye, darling,' said Mum, giving Lee a peck on the neck.

'I'll pick you and Britney up after school, on my way back from the scaredressers.'

Lee grabbed his cape and quickly dashed upstairs to brush his fangs and clean Britney's cage. Then he carefully carried it out to the van.

Britney was long, purple and legless, like a snake but with a pair of wings like a bat's. As they drove along, Lee poked his finger through the bars of the cage and tickled her under the chin. She flicked out her forked tongue and rattled her tail with pleasure.

Dad dropped Lee and
Britney off at the school gates.

'Bye, Lee,' he called as he
drove off. 'Have fun at show-
and-yell!'

'Thanks, Dad!' said Lee,
waving after him.

Just then a familiar gloomy voice droned, 'Fun! You vampires sink it is fun to fill my school with filthy, shtinky animals?'

It was old Eric Gore, the school's zombie caretaker.

'Who will have to clear up ze piles of pet poop, heh?' grouched Gore. 'Me!'

'Evening, Mr Gore,' said Lee politely. 'My pet's very clean actually. And she doesn't smell at all. Why don't you take a look at her?'

Lee held up Britney's cage and old Gore peered into it suspiciously. Britney suddenly flapped her wings, rattled her tail and gave a loud HISSS!!!

'Aargh!' shrieked Gore, jumping backwards in fright. 'You did zat on purpose!'

'Sorry,' said Lee innocently, trying not to laugh. 'She's fine when she gets to know you better, honest.'

'Just you votch out,' grumbled Gore. 'If I catch any animals loose in ze school I vill have you exshpelled!'

As old Gore lumbered off Lee looked in at his pet.

'Don't worry about that old grump, Britney,' he soothed. 'Everyone else is going to love you. I'm the only one in my class who's got a Battlesnake!'

Chapter 2
Pet Parade

In the classroom, Lee went
and sat next to his two best
friends, Billy Pratt and Bella
Williams.

'I can't wait for show-and-
yell!' said Billy. 'I've brought
along Cyril.'

In front of Billy stood a
fishbowl full of water. Inside
it was his pet, Cyril, a small
green scaly creature with four
legs, two fins, a big wide mouth
and a long orange bushy tail.

'I've brought Florence,' said Bella, carrying a small hutch. Her pet looked a bit like a rabbit except for its large black bat wings.

'And this is Britney, my new pet Battlesnake,' said Lee. But before he could open Britney's cage their teacher, Miss Gargoyle, walked in.

'Good evening, everyone!' she said. 'Quiet please. Before our show-and-yell I have an

important announcement.
Tonight St Orlok's is having
its annual visit from the Ghoul
Inspectors. So let's all be on
our best behaviour, shall we?'

'Yes, Miss Gargoyle,'
chorused
the class.

'Good.
And while
the Inspectors
are here all
your pets must be
kept locked in their cages or
hutches. There must be no

animals running or flying around the school. Except when we turn into bats, of course.'

Turning into a bat was one of the things Lee and his friends learned at vampire school. They also had lessons in lots of other vampire skills, like scary staring, turning your reflection off and on, and PE (Prowling Exercises).

'Right, let's get on with our show-and-yell,' said Miss Gargoyle. 'Who would like to go first?'

Two dozen hands shot high
into the air.

'We'll start with you, Billy,'
said Miss Gargoyle. 'What
have you brought to show us?'

'He's called Cyril,' said Billy.
'He's a Transylvanian Squish.

He's half squirrel and half
fish. He lives in water but I
have to let him out three times
a day for a run up a tree.'

'What do Squishes eat?'
asked Big Herb, one of Lee
and Billy's classmates. Eating
was Big Herb's favourite subject.

'Oh, just normal fish food,' said Billy. 'And acorns.'

'Thank you, Billy,' said Miss Gargoyle. 'Herbert, maybe you'd like to go next?'

Big Herb opened the hutch on his desk and took out a tiny ball of fur.

'This is Vernon,' said
Herb. 'He's a Dwarf Russian
Vampster.'

The creature yawned,
showing two very long
pointy fangs.

'And what do Vampsters eat?'
asked Bella.

'Leftovers,' said Herb.

'Leftovers?
In your house?'
piped up Lee.
'No wonder
Vernon looks hungry!'
Bella went next. Florence
flapped her wings, hopped high
into the air and did a double
somersault onto Bella's head.
Finally she
backflipped
onto the table
and took a
bow, to much
laughter
and clapping.

'Florence is a Funny Rabbit,' said Bella.

Then Lucy West brought out Violet, her Vampire Cat.

'Vampire Cats thleep all day and go out at night,' simpered Lucy. 'Jutht like us. Lots of Fangless people have Vampire Cats without even knowing it.'

Over the next two lessons the class saw Squishes and Vampsters, Mummy Bears and Vampire Cats, Funny Rabbits and Ghoulfish. At last Miss Gargoyle came to Lee.

'This is Britney, my new pet Battlesnake,' said Lee proudly, as he snapped on Britney's lead. 'Battlesnakes are half bat and half rattlesnake. They're really rare in this country.'

'Wow! Fab!' said Billy, as Britney flapped into the air. Lee gently pulled her back to

the table by
the lead.

'We got Britney
at the weekend from
the Monster Rescue Centre,'
said Lee. 'She was a stray. A
Fangless man found her in the
toilet. Or rather, Britney found
the man. Luckily her bite isn't
poisonous. He should be able

to sit down again in a day
or two.'

In the end, though, it wasn't
the Battlesnake that won the
prize for the creepiest pet.

Britney came joint second with
Grunter, Kitty Hognose's pet
Frankenswine, a three-eyed
piglet with a bolt through
its snout.

But the winner was Gussie,
Vlad Norris's pet. As soon
as the young vampires saw it
they all yelled in alarm. Billy

and one or two others were so
scared they turned into bats
and hid behind the curtains.

'We got it in a Fangless pet
shop,' said Vlad. 'It's called a
Guinea Pig.'

'Now that,' said Lee,
'is weird!'

Chapter 3
The Ghoul Inspectors

Just at that moment, the door flew open and in marched Mrs Garlick, the head teacher, with two ghouls they had never seen before. Both were carrying official-looking clipboards.

'Good morning, Miss Gargoyle,' said Mrs Garlick brightly. 'Allow me to introduce Mr Grinchley and Mrs Hat-Shep-Sut – the Ghoul Inspectors.'

The whole class stared at
the inspectors. Mr Grinchley
was a tall and gloomy vampire
in a pinstripe cape and a
bowler hat. Mrs Hat-Shep-
Sut was a short plump mummy
wearing large red glasses and a
bright purple velvet beret.

'He looks a right barrel of

laughs,' whispered Lee.

'I know,' agreed Billy. 'About as cheerful as old Gore.'

'The other one looks much jollier though,' said Bella.

'Mr Grinchley works for the Department of Deaducation,' said Mrs Garlick. 'Mrs Hat-Shep-Sut is visiting from abroad.

She wishes to find out about schools in this country. I'm afraid she doesn't speak a great deal of English.'

The mummy nodded and gave a little smile.

'Hat-Shep-Sut not chat much,' she chuckled.

Mr Grinchley grimaced grimly at the class. Then he spotted the hutches and cages.

'Most irregular,' said Mr Grinchley. 'They are all empty, I trust?'

He lifted Big Herb's hutch

and shook it.

'Tut-tut-tut, Meester Greenchley,' said the mummy. 'Hat-Shep-Sut think best not touch!'

Herb's Vampster gave a sharp and rather cross squeak. On the other side of the classroom Lucy West's Vampire Cat answered at once with a loud, hungry yowl. This set off the rest of the pets, who broke into a cacophony of yaps and grunts and screeches and squeaks and squawks.

'Tee-hee-hee, Meester Greenchley!' giggled the mummy. 'Hat-Shep-Sut said hands off hutch!'

'Animals!' wailed Mr Grinchley above the din. 'In class!

Most irregular!'

'We've been having a show-and-yell evening,' said Miss Gargoyle a little uncertainly. 'We've met lots of lovely creepy pets, haven't we, children?'

'Yes, Miss Gargoyle,' nodded the class.

'And what proper lessons have they missed for this – this show-and-yell?' asked Mr Grinchley glumly.

'Um ... maths mainly,' said Miss Gargoyle.

The mummy grinned at the class.

'Good, good, good!' she chortled. 'Hat-Shep-Sut hate sums much!'

Some of the class laughed too, until Mr Grinchley glared at them.

'Missing maths is no laughing matter, Mrs Hat-Shep-Sut,'

he grumbled. 'In fact it is most irregular.'

He scribbled a note furiously on his clipboard. Miss Gargoyle and Mrs Garlick swapped worried glances.

Just then the school bell rang.

'Ah, break time!' chirped Mrs Garlick. 'Come along, Mr Grinchley and Mrs Hat-Shep-Sut, why don't we go to the staff crypt for a coffee?'

'Ta very much!' said the mummy. 'Hat-Shep-Sut like nice big cup!'

'I only drink tea,' droned Mr Grinchley.

'A special tea called Count
Black. Two cups a day. Nice
and regular. But animals
in school are quite another
matter. They are irregular.
Most irregular indeed. If I
find one of these creatures
loose in the school its owner
will be expelled!'

'Well, we'll make sure our pets stay locked up during break, won't we children?' said Miss Gargoyle anxiously.

'Yes, Miss Gargoyle,' replied the class.

'Good!' said Mr Grinchley, with a suspicious eye on Billy's fishbowl, where Cyril the Squish had started splashing water noisily.

'Come along now, Mr Grinchley!' said Mrs Garlick

breezily, gripping him firmly by the arm. 'It's four minutes past eleven. I would be very upset if you missed your tea!'

As Mrs Garlick ushered the inspectors out of the classroom, Lee could have sworn she winked at Miss Gargoyle.

'I'll see you all after break,' sighed Miss Gargoyle. 'If you need me I'll be in the dining hall. I need a nice strong cup of coffee. But not in the staff crypt with Mr Grinchley!'

Chapter 4
Squish Squabble

'Phew!' said Lee. 'Saved by the bell! Mrs Hat-Hitch-Hotchpotch – or whatever it is seems nice but that Grinchley is a miserable old ghoul.'

'Yeah,' agreed Bella. 'Fancy thinking we'd let our pets run wild all over the school.'

There was a loud squeal from Cyril. The Squish had stopped splashing about but was now furiously thumping the lid of the bowl.

'Yikes!' said Billy. 'I really need to let Cyril out for a run. I also think he needs to – um – do his business, if you know what I mean.'

'But what if the Ghoul
Inspectors spot Cyril running
about?' said Bella. 'It would be
awful to get caught after what
Mr Grinchley just said.'

'Oh, don't worry about him,'
said Lee. 'He's down
in the staff
crypt
with Mrs
Garlick,
isn't he?
Come on!'

Billy hid Cyril's bowl under his cape and the three friends went outside. They slipped through the shadows to a great oak tree that grew in the grounds next to the school gates.

Lee and Bella checked no one was coming while Billy carefully took the lid off Cyril's bowl. The Squish climbed out and immediately shot up the tree. After a quick gleeful scurry about, he sat on a branch that stuck out over the school wall.

'Great,' smiled Billy. 'He's happy now.' 'But we mustn't be too long,' said Lee. 'How do you get him to come down again?'

'Oh, he always comes down as soon as he's done his you-know-what,' said Billy.

'And as long as no one shouts at him.'

'Why?' asked Bella. 'What happens?'

But before Billy could answer, a familiar voice hollered, 'Hey! You pesky vampire kids! Vot are you up to behind zat tree, eh?'

'Oh no, it's old Gore!' hissed Lee. 'And he's got Mrs Garlick and the Ghoul Inspectors with him!'

'Really, Mr Gore,' chirped Mrs Garlick. 'They are probably just playing hide-and-shriek. It is breaktime, after all.'

Lee, Billy and Bella smiled innocently, hoping that nobody would look up at Cyril, who was now happily nibbling an acorn.

'I know zese kids,' grumbled Gore. 'I'll bet zey are up to no good! OUCH!'

A large acorn had just bounced off old Gore's head,

dislodging several cornflake-size lumps of dandruff. To the children's dismay he looked up just in time to see Cyril sticking out his tongue and blowing a loud raspberry. THHRRRRRRUP!

'Ha!' roared Gore. 'I knew it! Look, zey have let an animal loose in ze school!'

'Is this true?' frowned Mrs Garlick.

'Yes, Mrs Garlick,' admitted Billy guiltily. 'It's mine.'

'Shockingly irregular!' exclaimed Mr Grinchley.

Old Gore was delighted.

'Ho ho! Exshpulsion for you!'

he crowed. Then he shook his fist at Cyril, showering Mr Grinchley with little green flakes of finger.

'And as for you,' he bellowed. 'Come down out of zat tree at vonce, you shtupid animal!'

Cyril frowned. Then he turned around on the branch so that Mr Gore was looking straight up at his rear end.

'Er ... I wouldn't shout at Cyril if I were you,' said Billy nervously. But old Gore ignored him.

'You ugly brute!' he shouted
more loudly. 'Get down
here NOW!'

Cyril slowly lifted his tail,
waggled his bottom and then …
SPLAT!

Everyone gawped at the
smelly brown mess all over
Mr Gore's face. Except for
Mr Grinchley they
all tried very
hard not to
laugh.

'Eee-uuw!' said Lee. 'So that's what happens when you shout at a Squish.'

Mr Gore glared at Billy.

'Vy, you – you pesky ...' he spluttered, spitting out a mouthful of Squish droppings. 'Zis boy must be punished!'

'Quite right!' griped Mr Grinchley. 'He has admitted letting his animal loose. He must be expelled!'

Billy looked gloomily at Lee and Bella. But Mrs Garlick was smiling.

'Well, Mr Grinchley,' she said cheerfully. 'You are quite right that it is forbidden to let an animal loose in the school. However, that creature isn't in the school.'

'Vot?' spluttered Gore. 'But ze tree is in ze school grounds!'

'Most of it is, I agree,' trilled

Mrs Garlick. 'But that branch isn't. It sticks out over the school wall. So actually the animal is not in the school at all. Isn't that so, Mr Grinchley?'

'Well-I-I,' stuttered the inspector. 'It is most irregular, but I suppose, technically ...'

'Excellent!' said Mrs Garlick breezily. 'Now, let's continue our tour of the school. Come along!'

As Mrs Garlick and the Ghoul Inspectors turned to go,

Cyril leapt from the branch back into his bowl, splashing water all over Mr Gore.

'Urgh!! Pesky kids!'

Old Gore lumbered off after the others.

Once he was out of earshot
the three friends burst out
laughing.

'Nice one, Cyril!'
chortled Lee.

It was then that they heard
the scream ...

Chapter 5
Toilet Trouble

'AAARRRGGGHHH!!!!'

Lee, Billy and Bella hurried back into the school. A small crowd of young vampires had gathered outside the girls' toilets. In the middle of the crowd was Lucy West. She was in hysterics.

'What is it, Lucy?' asked Lee. 'What's happened?'

To his dismay Lucy pointed at him and screeched, 'I'll tell you what'th happened, Lee Prithe! Your pethky pet jutht bit my bottom!'

'Britney?' gasped Lee. 'Loose in the loo? No way!'

'*Yeth* way!' snapped Lucy.

'You're the only perthon in the school who's got a Battlethnake!'

Lee's heart sank as he realised what had happened. In all the fuss over Cyril the Squish, he must have forgotten to lock Britney's cage!

'Eek! Sorry, Lucy,' he said. 'We'd better catch her before she bites anyone else!'

But the girls in the crowd all shook their heads.

'We're not going in there!' said Naz Patel. 'We don't want

to get bitten!'

Lee turned to Bella.

'Sorry, Lee,' she smiled. 'Britney knows you. I think it'll be much easier if you catch her yourself!'

'All right,' said Lee. 'But don't let any girls in till I've got her!'

Lee glanced down the corridor and when no one was in sight he quickly dashed through the door. Britney was curled up in one of the toilets. She happily rattled her tail when she saw Lee looking down at her.

'Hello, Britney,' he said, whipping off his cape and laying it on the floor. 'Bathtime's over.'

He stroked Britney's head and put his hands into the water.

'Ugh!' he winced. 'I hope someone's cleaned the loos this morning!'

Lee quickly picked up the sopping wet Battlesnake and laid her on his cape. Then he bundled her up before she could escape.

'Right,' he said. 'Now let's get you back in your cage before anyone sees you!'

With Britney under one arm Lee grabbed the door handle and hastily stepped out into the corridor.

'Phew!' he declared. 'I did it!' It was then he saw that the crowd had grown.

Standing in front of him
were old Gore, Mrs Garlick –
and the Ghoul Inspectors.

Chapter 6

Mummy Knows Best

'So,' declared Gore triumphantly. 'A boy in ze girls' toilets! It is against school rules! And vot is that under your arm?'

'Um, it's my cape,' said Lee.

'Ha! Another rule broken!'

droned Gore. 'School uniform must be vorn at all times!'

'Dear me, Mrs Garlick,' said Mr Grinchley. 'This is highly irregular – the boy has broken not one but two school rules!'

'Two rather minor rules,' sighed Mrs Garlick.

'Rules are rules!' snapped Mr Grinchley. 'I shall be putting this in my report!'

'Oh well,' thought Lee. 'At least they haven't found Britney.'

But old Gore hadn't finished. He had been eyeing Lee's cape suspiciously.

'Oh, I sink it is more than two small rules he has broken,' he smirked. 'Vot is inside your cape, boy?'

Lee's heart sank.

'Well, boy?' grumbled Grinchley. 'Let us see what you're hiding.'

Lee slowly unfolded his cape.

Britney lifted her head and stuck her tongue out at old Gore with a loud HISSS!!!

'Arrrghh!' screamed Lucy. 'That'th the beatht that bit my bum!'

'Ha! I knew it!' crowed Gore. 'A dangerous animal! It was on ze loose in ze toilet!'

'Is this true, Lee?' said Mrs Garlick sternly. 'Is this your animal?'

Lee nodded sadly, putting

his cape back on.

'Sorry, Mrs Garlick.'

'Shockingly irregular!' grouched Grinchley. 'As I said before, Mrs Garlick, there is only one punishment for letting a creature loose in school. The owner must be expelled!'

'Yes! Yes!' gloated Gore.

'Exshpel him! Exshpel him!'

'Stop! Hat-Shep-Sut say wait a sec!'

cried Mrs Hat-Shep-Sut.
She was looking carefully at
Britney. 'Brenda!' she declared
suddenly. 'Come to Mummy!'

The Battlesnake flew at once
into her arms.

'Votch out!' hollered Gore.
'It's attacking her!'

'No!' said the mummy. 'Hat-Shep-Sut say keep trap shut! This my pet!'

Everybody gasped.

'What!' said Lee. 'Your pet?'

'Yes,' beamed Mrs Hat-Shep-Sut. 'Lost last week. Me miss very much!'

Britney – or rather Brenda – nuzzled Mrs Hat-Shep-Sut and shook her tail affectionately.

'Oh,' said Lee in dismay. 'So she wasn't a stray after all.'

'It makes no difference!' groused Grinchley. 'The boy

must be expelled!'

'But I'm afraid
that's quite impossible
Mr Grinchley!' Mrs
Garlick said firmly.

'What?' exclaimed
Grinchley. 'The
school rules are perfectly clear.
The owner of any animal on
the loose shall be expelled!'

'Yes, indeed,' said Mrs
Garlick brightly. 'But the
owner of this
animal is not
Lee Price.

It is Mrs Hat-Shep-Sut. Isn't that so, Lee?'

'Yes, I suppose so,' he sighed.

'There you are. Mrs Hat-Shep-Sut is not a pupil at the school,' chirped Mrs Garlick. 'So how can I expel her?'

'But-but ...' spluttered Grinchley. 'This is most irregular!'

'Splendid! I'm glad we've sorted that out,' warbled Mrs Garlick. 'Now then, the Inspectors and I are going to listen to a rehearsal of the

Ghoul Orchestra. Mr Gore, I'm sure you've got work to attend to, so please don't let us keep you.'

Gore stomped off, grunting something that included 'pesky vampires' and one or two other words that are too rude to write down.

Mrs Hat-Shep-Sut went over to Lee. When the Battlesnake saw him it lifted its head and rattled its tail in pleasure.

'Hat-Shep-Sut bring pet say bye,' said the mummy.

'Bye-bye, Britney, I mean Brenda,' said Lee sadly, stroking the Battlesnake.

'Never mind, Lee,' said Bella kindly. 'You can always get another pet.'

'I suppose so,' said Lee. 'It's just that Battlesnakes are so very rare.'

'No, no, no!' smiled the mummy. 'Boy make mistake! Pet not say bye to boy but bye to Hat-Shep-Sut!'

She gently handed the Battlesnake to Lee.

'Er – what are you doing?' asked Lee.

'Hat-Shep-Sut hate see chap upset,' said the mummy. 'Boy cheer up. Hat-Shep-Sut give boy back pet!'

'Really?' grinned Lee. 'Are you sure? Won't you miss her?'

'Yes, yes, yes,' smiled the mummy. 'But Mrs Hat-Shep-Sut have six more!'

She leaned over and tickled the Battlesnake under the

chin. It rattled its tail and snuggled up to Lee.

'See!' said the mummy. 'Boy

happy, pet happy, so Mrs Hat-Shep-Sut happy. Bye-bye, Brenda, I mean bye-bye, Britney!'

'Thanks!' said Lee. 'Mrs Hat-Shop – Hot-Chip – Ketchup ...'

'Call me Hattie!' giggled Mrs Hat-Shep-Sut.

'Now, my dears,' said Mrs Garlick to the crowd of young vampires. 'The bell is about to go for lessons, so run along back to your classrooms.'

As the head led the Ghoul

Inspectors away, she turned
to Lee.

'Oh, and Lee Price,' she said.

'Yes, Mrs Garlick?' said Lee.

'Do keep your cape on, my
dear,' said Mrs Garlick. 'And
try to stay out of the
girls' toilets!'

The End